BUG-NAPPED

Don't miss any of the cases in the Hardy Boys Clue Book series!

HARDY BOYS

→ Clue Book ←

#11

BUG-NAPPED

BY FRANKLIN W. DIXON ⇄ ILLUSTRATED BY SANTY GUTIÉRREZ

ALADDIN

NEW YORK LONDON TORONTO SYDNEY NEW DELHI

ALADDIN

An imprint of Simon & Schuster Children's Publishing Division
1230 Avenue of the Americas, New York, NY 10020
First Aladdin paperback edition April 2020
Text copyright © 2020 by Simon & Schuster, Inc.
Illustrations copyright © 2020 by Santy Gutiérrez
Also available in an Aladdin hardcover edition.
All rights reserved, including the right of reproduction in whole or in part in any form.
ALADDIN and related logo are registered trademarks of Simon & Schuster, Inc.
THE HARDY BOYS and colophons are registered trademarks of Simon & Schuster, Inc.
HARDY BOYS CLUE BOOK and colophons are trademarks of Simon & Schuster, Inc.
For information about special discounts for bulk purchases, please contact
Simon & Schuster Special Sales at 1-866-506-1949 or business@simonandschuster.com.
The Simon & Schuster Speakers Bureau can bring authors to your live event.
For more information or to book an event contact the Simon & Schuster Speakers Bureau
at 1-866-248-3049 or visit our website at www.simonspeakers.com.
Series designed by Karina Granda
Cover designed by Tiara Iandiorio
The text of this book was set in Adobe Garamond Pro.
Manufactured in the United States of America 0320 OFF
2 4 6 8 10 9 7 5 3 1
Library of Congress Cataloging-in-Publication Data
Names: Dixon, Franklin W., author. | Gutiérrez, Santy, illustrator.
Title: Bug-napped! / by Franklin W. Dixon ; illustrated by Gutiérrez.
Description: First Aladdin hardcover/paperback edition. | New York : Aladdin, [2019] | Series: Hardy boys clue book ; 11 | Summary: "Detective brothers Frank and Joe search for a very special beetle"—Provided by publisher. | Identifiers: LCCN 2019003754 (print) | LCCN 2019006266 (eBook) | ISBN 9781534431287 (eBook) | ISBN 9781534431263 (pbk) | ISBN 9781534431270 (hardcover)
Subjects: | CYAC: Lost and found possessions—Fiction. |
Beetles—Fiction. | Brothers—Fiction. | Mystery and detective stories.
Classification: LCC PZ7.D644 (eBook) | LCC PZ7.D644 Bug 2020 (print) | DDC [Fic]—dc23
LC record available at https://lccn.loc.gov/2019003754

CONTENTS

BUG-NAPPED

EARTH TO HARDYS

"Remind me why there's kale on my pizza, Frank," eight-year-old Joe Hardy said, holding a slice topped with the leafy veggie, "and not pepperoni or meatballs?"

"Because it's an Earth Day Festival in the park, Joe," nine-year-old Frank Hardy reminded his brother. "Everything on the scene is green."

"That's for sure." Joe sighed, staring at the grassy-looking slice.

"Besides," said Frank, "eating healthy is a good idea before the Globe Gut Belly Bump."

Joe smiled at the mention of the contest he would compete in soon. He couldn't wait to wear a giant inflated globe around his middle and bump his challenger until one of them dropped to the mat. As if that wasn't cool enough, Joe and his fellow bump contestant were signed up to go first!

"Who's your opponent, Joe?" Frank asked.

"Coach Lambert told me his name is Aki Kubo," Joe said. "Aki moved here with his parents from Japan. That's practically the other side of the world!"

"Well, it is Earth Day!" said Frank.

Joe was about to try a bite of his pizza when he felt something tug at his slice. Turning, he saw his pizza halfway inside the mouth of a robot!

"Hey!" Joe cried. "The robot's eating my pizza!"

He and Frank tried to pull the pizza slice from the sucking jaws of the capsule-shaped machine, but it was no use.

"Munchy is hungry," the robot droned. "Feed me pizza crusts, banana peels, watermelon seeds—"

"Munchy, no!" a voice called out.

The brothers turned to see their friend Phil Cohen racing over. Phil flipped a switch on the robot, stopping his chomping at once.

"Thanks, Phil," Joe said, although his pizza slice was a goner.

"Is Munchy one of your inventions, Phil?" asked Frank.

Phil nodded proudly. Everyone knew he was the best inventor at Bayport Elementary School. "You bet," he said. "I invented Munchy for the Earth Day Junior Inventors Challenge tomorrow."

"A robot that eats pizza?" Joe cried.

"Munchy chews up leftover scraps and turns them into compost," Phil explained. "Compost is great for the soil."

"So that's where my pizza slice is going," Joe sighed. "In the dirt!"

"Sorry, Joe," Phil said. "I have to reprogram Munchy to eat only scraps."

"Or maybe just the kale topping on a pizza," Joe joked.

Phil gazed at his robot. "I have to win tomorrow, you guys," he said. "First prize is a whole summer at a camp for kid inventors. I'd do anything to go to Camp Galileo. Anything!"

"You'll win, Phil," Frank insisted. "Munchy is awesome!"

"You should see the inventions I'm up against!" Phil groaned. "A straw that turns swamp water into fresh water! A scooter made from recycled plastic bottles! There'll even be a fake leather jacket made out of chewed-up bubble-gum wads."

"Wow!" Joe said, his eyes wide.

"Good luck tomorrow, Phil," said Frank.

"Thanks," Phil sighed. "I'm sure going to need it!"

He flipped another switch on his robot. Then he walked away, with Munchy following behind him. The tip of Joe's pizza slice was sticking out of the robot's mouth.

"Munchy may have eaten my pizza, Frank," Joe said. "But at least he didn't eat something way more important."

"What?" Frank asked.

"Our clue book!" said Joe with a grin.

"You brought our clue book here?" Frank asked. "To an Earth Day celebration?"

Joe patted his jacket pocket. "I bring our clue book everywhere!" he declared.

That was because Frank and Joe loved solving mysteries. Their clue book was where they wrote all their clues, suspects, and most important, the five questions good detectives ask themselves: *who, what, where, when,* and *why?*

"You won't need our clue book during the Globe Gut Belly Bump Contest," Frank said. "Let's see what else is going on around here before the contest starts."

The brothers walked through the festival, seeing lots of Earth Day activities. There was a crafts table where kids made bugs and flowers out of wire. One booth sold organic cupcakes, while another handed out free samples of bright green smoothies. Joe was pretty sure they had kale in them!

As they walked on, Frank and Joe spotted a man pinning a flyer to a tree. The buggy antennas he wore on his head bobbed as he worked. After the man walked away, the brothers checked out the flyer.

"'Carl the Critter Curator's Insectarium,'" Joe read out loud. He turned to Frank and asked, "What's a curator?"

"Someone who finds things for museums," Frank replied. "We met one on our class trip to the Bayport Museum of Natural History."

"So if Carl is a critter curator, that means he finds bugs!" Joe said excitedly. "The flyer says it's a museum for live insects. Cool!"

The picture on the front showed Carl holding a giant caterpillar. The boys realized that he was the man they'd just seen putting up the flyer. In the picture, he wore the same purple antennas as he grinned from ear to ear.

"It says to bring the kids," said Frank, pointing to the flyer.

"Yeah," Joe chuckled. "And bug spray!"

The brothers were turning away from the tree when—

"Out of my way, out of my way!" a voice shouted.

The voice belonged to the Hardys' seven-year-old neighbor, Lester Lopez. Lester was wearing his Tadpole Scout uniform as he hurried to catch up with his sniffing beagle.

"Hi, Lester," Joe said. "Why is your dog sticking his nose in everything?"

Lester tugged his dog's leash to make him stop. "Mr. Sniff is a scent hound," he explained. "He's sniffing for things on my Tadpole Scout scavenger hunt list."

"A scavenger hunt?" said Joe. "What's the prize?"

"A new Tadpole Scout badge!" Lester said. He handed Mr. Sniff's leash to Joe, then pointed to the other badges on his uniform. "I got this badge for cheese making, this one for trash recycling, this for sock balling—"

"Woof!" Mr. Sniff barked, before zooming off.

"Whoa!" Joe shouted, still holding the leash as the beagle pulled him across the grass. "I think Mr. Sniff just caught a whiff!"

Joe stumbled after Mr. Sniff, gripping the leash

with both hands. He was relieved when the bounding beagle stopped short at a boy holding a plant. Joe recognized the boy. He was Leif Bloomquist, from his third-grade class.

Leif had the best name for someone who loved plants. He even had a weekend job delivering the *Bayport Penny Pincher*. It helped to pay for seeds and new gardening tools.

"Get this dog away from Jaws!" Leif shouted as Mr. Sniff jumped up on him.

"Get your plant away from my dog!" Lester shouted back, grabbing the leash from Joe.

Frank, Joe, and Leif watched Lester walk off with Mr. Sniff, still sniffing everything in his path.

"Is your plant okay, Leif?" Frank asked.

"Shh—don't call him a plant," Leif said as if it could hear. "His name is Jaws, and he's a Venus flytrap."

"Flytrap?" asked Joe. "Does he eat flies?"

"Mostly bugs that crawl," Leif said. "Like these guys."

From his pocket Leif pulled out a small jar filled

with insects, unscrewed it, and shook out one of the bugs. The brothers watched wide-eyed as Leif placed the bug between two spiky leaves of the plant. The leaves closed over the bug and swallowed it whole.

"Whoa!" Joe exclaimed.

"That plant really is a trap!" said Frank.

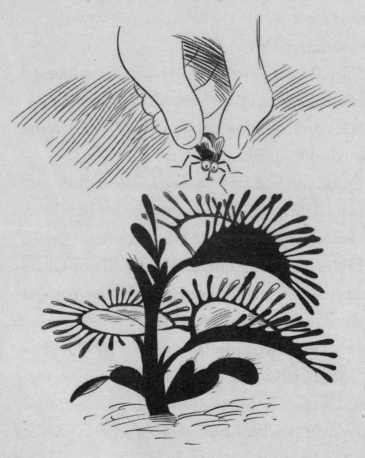

"I just wish I had bigger bugs to feed him," Leif said. "Like a beetle or a tarantula, so Jaws's leaves wouldn't be so pale and droopy."

The brothers watched Leif walk away, holding Jaws carefully.

"Jaws seemed to have a healthy appetite to me!" Joe said.

Suddenly—

"The Globe Gut Belly Bump Contest will begin in ten minutes," a voice boomed across the loudspeaker. "Will all belly bumpers please come to the game mat right away?"

"Frank, this is it!" Joe said excitedly.

"Bust a gut, Joe!" said Frank. "You got this!"

Joe raced ahead of Frank to the game mat. Placed side by side on the mat were the two inflated Globe Guts. A boy was kneeling at one end of the mat. Joe also saw Coach Lambert, from Bayport Elementary School, waiting by the inflated globes. He would be judging the contest.

"Ready to go first, Joe?" Coach Lambert reminded him.

"Ready as spaghetti, Coach!" Joe said with a thumbs-up. "Is that Aki Kubo?"

"Yes, there he is!" Coach Lambert said. He pointed to the kneeling boy, who was whispering softly to something on the ground covered with a white cloth.

What's under there? Joe wondered. *And why is Aki talking to it?*

Chapter
2

GOOD-LUCK SWARM

"Ready, Aki?" Coach Lambert asked.

Aki stood up and nodded. "Ready, Coach!" he said.

Joe and Aki shook hands, then slipped into their huge inflated Globe Guts. Frank cheered for Joe from the crowd with Phil and Munchy. The robot had been programmed to cheer for Joe too . . . almost.

"Go, Joe!" Munchy droned. "Munchy is hungry. . . ."

"Okay, Joe and Aki, here are the rules," Coach Lambert said. "You can bump each other with your Globe Guts, but no using hands!"

Joe and Aki traded grins. The Globe Guts were so huge, they couldn't reach a thing!

"Ready . . . set . . . bump!" Coach Lambert shouted. He blew a whistle and stepped way back.

BUMP! BUMP! BUMP!

The crowd cheered for both Aki and Joe as they jumped and bumped. Each bump caused the boys to bounce back practically through the air. Both boys put up a good clash until Aki landed one enormous bump and—

"Oof!" Joe grunted as he fell back on the mat. He and his Globe Gut rolled and rolled until coming to a complete stop.

"And the winner is Aki Kubo!" Coach Lambert shouted, "Good job, you guys!"

Joe tried standing but kept rolling instead. "Thanks, Coach," he grunted. "Uh . . . can somebody help me up? Please?"

The coach pulled Joe to his feet. When both boys were out of their Globe Guts, they shook hands again.

"What's your secret, Aki?" asked Coach Lambert.

"I'll show you, Coach," Aki said.

He walked to the end of the mat, where his covered object stood. Aki whipped off the cover to reveal a small tank underneath. Joe was near enough to see what was inside. It was a big black bug with lots of legs!

Aki popped off the lid and lifted the bug out of the tank. Shouts of "Awesome," "Whoa!" and "Eww!" rose from the crowd.

"Meet Izumi, a stag beetle," Aki explained. "Many kids in Japan have stag beetles as pets."

Joe pointed to Izumi. "He looks like he's wearing a samurai helmet," he said.

"That's why some call them samurai beetles," Aki said. "They're also good luck, which is why I brought Izumi here today."

Frank could hear Phil gasp, "That bug is good luck? No way!"

"Well, Aki," Coach Lambert said. "If stag beetles are good luck, then Izumi certainly did his job."

As the winner, Aki received a bicycle helmet. Joe won a prize too, a gift card to a veggie burger place in Bayport.

"I hear their kale burgers are excellent," the coach told Joe.

"Kale, huh?" Joe gulped as he took the card. "Thanks . . . Coach Lambert."

Frank hurried over to Joe and Aki as they stepped away from the mat. While the next contestants got ready to bump, the brothers checked out Izumi in the palm of Aki's hand.

"Cool bug, Aki," said Frank.

"I don't know anyone with a bug for a pet," Joe admitted.

"Stag beetles make excellent pets," Aki said as he held out his bug. "Why don't you both take Izumi home and see for yourself?"

Frank and Joe exchanged surprised looks. Had they just heard what they thought they'd heard?

"You'd let us borrow Izumi?" Frank asked.

"But he's yours, Aki," said Joe.

"I know," Aki said, petting Izumi's wings. "But you seem like you will take good care of him."

"We will!" Frank said.

"For sure!" added Joe.

"Great, then," Aki said. "Just tell me where you live and I'll pick Izumi up on Sunday afternoon."

Frank told him their address, and then Aki slipped Izumi into the tank and secured the lid. He handed the tank to Joe.

"Thanks, Aki," Joe said. "What should we feed this big guy?"

"Beetles love fruit," replied Aki. He turned to see his family waving from a distance. "I have to go now. Have fun with Izumi, and I'll see you on Sunday!"

The brothers waved good-bye to Aki, then high-fived.

"A samurai stag beetle!" Joe cheered. "Are we lucky or what?"

"It's only for the weekend, Joe," Frank reminded him, "Let's take Izumi home and introduce him to Mom and Dad."

But as they left the festival, Joe had a feeling they were being followed. Glancing over his shoulder, he saw Carl the Critter Curator, still wearing his purple buggy antennas.

Carl was looking straight at Frank and Joe as he spoke on his phone: "I just had the most fabulous idea for our insectarium—a huge beetle!"

Joe smiled at Izumi inside the tank. "Hear that, Izumi?" he asked. "You're not just an insect. You're an inspiration!"

"A stag beetle?" Mr. Hardy asked.

"You brought a giant insect home for the weekend?" said Mrs. Hardy, staring at Izumi's tank on the kitchen counter.

"It's only temporary," Frank explained. "Think of it as a sleepover."

"Or as bugs would say," Joe joked, "a creep-over."

"Very funny," said Mr. Hardy with a grin.

Aunt Trudy was also in the kitchen, pulling a tray of fresh-baked cookies from the oven. The cookies were shaped like flowers, butterflies, and bugs!

"I have nothing against insects, boys," Aunt Trudy said as she placed the tray on the kitchen table. "Just keep that beetle away from my Earth Day cookies."

"I'll keep Izumi away," Joe said, reaching for a cookie. "As for me—"

"Don't even think about it, Joe Hardy," Aunt

Trudy cut in. "These cookies are for my special Earth Day book club meeting tonight. We're reading *The Great Gnatsby!*"

"Why don't you take Izumi upstairs, guys?" Mr. Hardy suggested.

"Can I bring him to my room?" asked Joe.

"As long as you keep him in your room," Mrs. Hardy said firmly. "As you can see, we're not the biggest fans of bugs yet. But maybe he would like a snack?"

Mrs. Hardy cut up some few apple slices to give to Izumi. While they popped the slices into Izumi's tank, Aunt Trudy said, "He's quiet now, but bugs can get pretty noisy."

"That's okay, Aunt Trudy," Joe said. "So can I!"

But that night, while Joe lay in bed, he learned what Aunt Trudy meant. Izumi's hissing and chirps were keeping him wide awake!

He rolled over to look at his bedside clock. It was ten thirty. He climbed out of bed and walked over to Izumi's tank on his desk.

"I can put you somewhere else in the house,

Izumi," Joe said. "But you'd only keep the others awake. Unless . . ."

He picked up the tank. ". . . I put you outside the house!"

Leaving his room, Joe cradled Izumi's tank in his arms.

The house was dark, but the stairs were always lit with a night-light. After heading downstairs, Joe carried Izumi's tank to the front door, opened it, and stepped outside. The warm spring day had turned into a chilly spring night.

"There you go, Izumi," Joe said, carefully placing the tank on the doorstep. "Now you can hiss like it's nobody's business!"

He went upstairs and back to bed, where he got a good night's sleep. The next morning he woke up early for a Saturday, and the house was quiet. Still in his pj's, Joe hurried downstairs to bring Izumi inside.

"Good morning, Izumi!" he said, pulling the front door open. He glanced down at the doorstep and gasped, then began to shout, "Frank, Frank! Izumi was hissing—and now he's missing!"

Chapter 3

INSECT INVESTIGATION

"What do you mean Izumi is missing, Joe?" Frank demanded. He was also in his pj's, having just been awakened by Joe's yells.

"Izumi was noisy last night, so I put his tank outside right here," Joe cried, pointing to the doorstep. "Now Izumi and his tank are gone!"

"Okay, okay," said Frank, trying to calm Joe down. "Let's ask Mom and Dad. Maybe they brought Izumi inside this morning."

But when the brothers asked their parents, they said they didn't know where Izumi was. So Frank and Joe called up to Aunt Trudy's window. She didn't have a clue either!

"Great," Joe groaned, as he and Frank returned to the empty doorstep. "I promised Aki we'd take care of his pet. What will I tell him when he comes for Izumi tomorrow afternoon?"

"Tomorrow afternoon means we have a whole day and half to find out who took Izumi," Frank pointed out.

"Took?" Joe asked, his eyebrows flying up. "You mean Izumi was . . . bug-napped?"

"Maybe," said Frank. "Go inside and get our clue book so we can open this case."

"Our clue book?" Joe reached into the pocket of his pj's and said, "Got it!"

"In your pajamas?" Frank asked.

"I told you, Frank," said Joe with a grin. "I carry our clue book everywhere. Even to bed!"

The brothers sat on the doorstep. Joe opened the clue book to a fresh page. Using the pen tucked inside the book, he wrote the five *W*s: *who*, *what*, *where*, *when*, and *why*.

"Let's start with *what*, as in what happened," Joe said. "Izumi was on our doorstep last night. This morning he's gone."

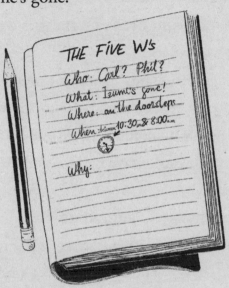

While Joe wrote in the clue book, Frank said, "*Where* is the doorstep. But *when* did the crime take place?"

"It was ten thirty when I took Izumi outside last night," said Joe. He drew a small clock on the page, with its hands on ten thirty.

"It was eight o'clock when you went outside for Izumi," Frank said.

"How do you know?" Joe asked.

"I looked at the clock when your yelling woke me up," said Frank with a frown. "Ten thirty at night until just before eight in the morning is a pretty big timeline."

Joe shrugged and said, "Izumi is a pretty big bug!"

The brothers studied the page to see what they had so far. Frank pointed to *where* and said, "Who-ever took Izumi would have had to come straight up to our house."

"A creepy thought," Joe admitted.

"Which brings us to our next *W*," Frank said. "*Who* would have snatched an insect and run off with it?"

The word "insect" made Joe's eyes light up. Insect . . . Insectarium . . . Carl!

"That guy Carl the Critter Curator followed us after I got Izumi!" Joe said. "He was on his phone, too, talking to someone about getting a beetle for his insectarium!"

"How would Carl know where we lived?" asked Frank. "I'm pretty sure he didn't follow us home."

"Pretty sure isn't sure-sure," Joe said.

"We have no proof Carl took Izumi either," Frank pointed out. "And Dad always tells us not to accuse anyone until we have proof."

"We're not *accusing* Carl," Joe said as he started the suspect list with the critter curator. "We're *suspecting* him!"

Frank still wasn't sold on Carl. "Okay, even if Carl knows where we live," he said, "how would he know that you put Izumi outside?"

Joe shrugged his shoulders and said, "Maybe he got here and lucked out."

"Luck!" Frank said, his eyes wide.

"What about it?" asked Joe.

"Phil wanted luck to win the Junior Inventors Challenge today," Frank explained. "Remember how interested he was when Aki said Izumi was his lucky bug?"

"Phil also said he'd do anything to go to Camp Galileo," Joe said. "And he knows where we live because he's our friend."

"He could have come by early this morning to ask us for Izumi," Frank said. "And saw him on our doorstep instead."

Joe was about to include Phil on the suspect list, but then he shook his head. "You know we don't like suspecting our friends, Frank," he said. "And Phil wouldn't steal anything from us."

"I know," Frank agreed. "Unless Phil wanted Camp Galileo so bad he wasn't thinking."

Joe heaved a sigh as he added Phil to the suspect list. "Two suspects are a good start," he said after shutting the clue book and standing up. "Let's go inside, get dressed, and have breakfast."

"Good idea," Frank said. "Then we'll look around the yard for clues."

Joe was about to open the door when he spotted something lying against the side of the doorstep. "Uh . . . Frank?" he said, "I think I just found one."

"Found what?" asked Frank.

Joe smiled as he said, "A clue!"

PLANT A CLUE

"What clue, Joe?" Frank asked. "Footprints?"

"Nope," said Joe. He lifted a rolled up newspaper and held it up. "The *Bayport Penny Pincher*!"

Frank wrinkled his nose in confusion. "What about the *Penny Pincher*?" he asked, "It gets delivered every Saturday morning."

"And who delivers it every Saturday morning?" Joe asked. "Leif Bloomquist!"

Frank remembered seeing Leif at the Earth Day Festival. He also remembered what Leif had told them about Jaws.

"Leif wanted a big bug for his Venus flytrap," Frank recalled. "Something like a tarantula or a beetle."

"A beetle like Izumi!" Joe added. "If Leif was here early to deliver the *Penny Pincher*, he would have seen the tank right here!"

The brothers were about to high-five their latest discovery, when their hands froze midair.

"Um . . . Joe," Frank said. "If Leif took Izumi for Jaws, you know what that means."

"Izumi was breakfast!" Joe cried. "What will we tell Aki?"

"Take a deep breath," said Frank. "Just because Leif is a suspect doesn't mean he took Izumi to feed Jaws!"

"Then what do we do?" asked Joe.

"We question Leif," Frank said. "And look for Izumi's tank. If it's empty, we'll know what happened."

"Yeah," Joe groaned. "Plant chow."

Joe wrote Leif Bloomquist's name in their clue book, but quickly. If they were going to save Izumi from the jaws of Jaws, they'd have to act fast. After the boys got dressed and ate a super-quick breakfast, Joe found Leif's name and address on his class roster. The brothers told their mom where they were going, and then they practically ran toward the Bloomquist house. Until—

"Frank, Joe!" a voice called.

The brothers turned. Their mouths dropped open when they saw—

"Aki!" Joe gasped.

"W-what's up?" Frank stammered.

Aki wore his prize helmet as he rode his scooter up to the brothers. "How's Izumi doing?" he asked.

"Why?" Frank blurted. "You don't want him back, do you?"

"Not yet," Aki said. "I do miss Izumi, but it's okay that you keep him until tomorrow." He tilted his head curiously. "Why isn't Izumi with you?"

he asked. "I carry his tank practically everywhere I go."

Joe thought quickly. "Uh—Izumi wouldn't want to go where we're going!"

"Where are you going?" Aki asked.

"To a friend's house," answered Joe. "He's got a pet that eats bugs."

"A pet that eats bugs . . . ," Aki said slowly. Then his eyes lit up. "Is it a bearded dragon or a gecko? Can I come too and see it?"

"Not a good idea, Aki!" said Frank quickly.

"Gecky is very shy!" Joe added. "See you tomorrow!"

The brothers left Aki on his scooter and charged ahead to Leif's house.

"'Gecky'?" asked Frank.

"You come up with a better gecko name, Frank," Joe complained. "Of all the kids to run into today. What will we tell Aki if Jaws really did eat—"

"Quit it, Joe!" Frank cut in. "Let's hope for the best."

The brothers reached Leif's house, where Mrs. Bloomquist was struggling to pull a thick magazine out of the mailbox.

"Are you boys here to see Leif?" she asked cheerily. "He's running an errand at the gardening store."

Frank and Joe traded looks. If Leif wasn't home, maybe they could look for clues.

"Actually, Mrs. Bloomquist," Frank said, "we're here to visit Jaws."

Mrs. Bloomquist turned from the mailbox to look at the brothers. "You mean Leif's Venus flytrap?" she asked. "Why do you want to visit him?"

"We heard he wasn't feeling well," Joe explained. "So we're paying a sick call."

"Oh, that's nice," Mrs. Bloomquist said with a smile. "But Leif told me Jaws is feeling much better today."

"Why?" Joe asked, almost afraid to hear the answer.

"Leif fed Jaws a big bug this morning and he

perked up," Mrs. Bloomquist said. "But if you still want to see Jaws, he's in the back."

Frank and Joe nodded slowly, too stunned to speak. Was the big bug that Leif had fed Jaws . . . Izumi?

The brothers walked glumly around the house to the backyard. They expected to see a few plants on a table or in a garden. Instead they found a whole greenhouse filled with dozens of plants.

"Just our luck," Joe groaned. "With all those plants, how are we going to find Jaws?"

"Don't look for Jaws," Frank said. "Look for Izumi."

Entering the greenhouse, the brothers split up to search for Izumi's tank. Frank checked out all kinds of potted plants, some with budding flowers, others that looked like miniature trees.

He was about to check out a thorny cactus when Joe's voice shouted from the other end of the greenhouse. . . .

"Frank! I found a Venus flytrap!"

Frank couldn't see Joe through all the high and

thick leaves. "How do you know it's a Venus fly-trap?" he called out to his brother.

"Because," shouted Joe, "it just trapped my finger!!"

Chapter 5

UP A TREE

Frank zigzagged through the maze of plants, following Joe's yells. He found his brother with his finger in between the jaws of Jaws!

"What happened?" Frank demanded.

"I wanted to look for traces of beetle in Jaws's mouth," said Joe, "so I stuck my finger in his trap and it snapped!"

"Joe, you're not a tiny bug," Frank said calmly. "Just pull your finger out."

Joe drew his finger out, easily and in one piece. "That wasn't so bad," he said. "And we found Jaws!"

"Look what else I found," said Frank.

Joe looked to see where Frank was pointing. There on the table next to Jaws was a bag labeled DR. BUGSBY'S GIANT FREEZE-DRIED INSECTS.

Frank lifted the clear plastic bag and said, "There are bugs in here that look like beetles. Dried-up beetles about the same size as Izumi."

"Do you think that's what Jaws ate for breakfast?" Joe asked hopefully. "Instead of Izumi?"

"Maybe," Frank said. "If we don't find his tank, then—"

WHOOOSH!!

Frank stopped midsentence as he and Joe yelped. Suddenly it was pouring inside the greenhouse!

Drenched from head to toe, Frank and Joe made their way through the plant jungle to the greenhouse door. Standing at the entrance was Leif. He was dressed in rubber boots and a canvas gardening hat. In his hand was something that looked like a remote.

"Leif, what did you do?" Joe cried.

"I'm using the overhead sprinkler system to water my plants," said Leif. "What were you doing in my greenhouse?"

"Your mom said it was okay to go in," Frank explained. "We wanted to visit Jaws."

"Why?" Leif asked.

"We're looking for a missing beetle," Joe said. "But all we found were bagged bugs."

"You mean Dr. Bugsby's Giant Freeze-Dried Insects?" Leif asked with a smile. "Aren't they great? I got them at the pet store yesterday, and Jaw loves them."

He glanced down at his remote and said, "I think that's enough water for today."

While Leif turned off the sprinklers, Frank and Joe turned away to talk privately.

"Just because Jaws eats dried beetles," whispered Frank, "doesn't mean he didn't eat a fresh beetle too."

"The crispy beetles could have been the appetizer," Joe whispered back, "with Izumi the main course."

"What are you guys whispering about?" Leif asked.

"We want to know if you saw anything on our

doorstep this morning," Frank replied, "when you were delivering the *Penny Pincher*."

"If you think I saw your missing beetle, the answer is no," Leif said. "Besides, I didn't deliver the *Penny Pincher* this morning."

"You didn't?" asked Frank.

"How come?" Joe added.

Leif pulled off his hat to reveal a wild and spiky haircut. "I was at barber Lou's shop so I asked my cousin to deliver them for me," he said. "I wanted to cut my hair to look like my favorite spider plant. What do you think?"

Joe studied Leif's haircut. If spider plants looked like spiders, then Lou had definitely nailed it. "Cool, Leif," Joe said, "but how do you get your hair to stick up like that?"

"With this!" answered Leif. He pulled a small tube from his jacket pocket. "Lou sold my dad this. It's some kind of gunk to keep my hair spiky."

Frank and Joe both wondered if Leif was telling the truth. Had he really gotten his hair cut this morning instead of delivering papers?

Just as Leif was about to pocket his hair gel,
Frank saw something wrapped around the tube. "Is
that a receipt, Leif?" he asked. "Can we see it?"

Leif pulled the receipt off the tube and handed it
to Frank. As the brothers studied the receipt, Frank
found what he was looking for.

"The date stamped on the receipt is today," Frank said in a low voice. "The time stamp is nine o'clock in the morning."

"If Leif was at the barber this morning," Joe whispered, "he couldn't have been delivering *Penny Pinchers*."

"Duh!" Leif said. "Next time don't bother whispering. I could hear every word!"

He took the receipt from Frank. "Now do you believe I didn't take that beetle?" he asked.

"Yes," said Frank. "Thanks for being a good sport."

"And for letting us see your greenhouse," Joe added with a smile. "I learned a lot!"

"Like what?" asked Leif.

"Like I'll eat kale over freeze-dried bugs any day!" Joe chuckled.

The brothers left the Bloomquist house to walk home, stopping on the way to cross Leif's name off the suspect list.

"I just remembered something," Frank said. "We promised Mom and Dad we'd pull weeds out of the grass today."

Joe sighed as he shut the clue book. "It is spring," he said. "And spring means spring chores."

Once home, Frank and Joe nibbled on leftover cookies from Aunt Trudy's book club meeting. Then they went outside and started yanking straggly weeds from the front lawn.

"After we do this," Frank grunted as he struggled with a stubborn dandelion, "let's go to Phil's house and ask him some questions."

Joe frowned as he worked on some weeds around a tree. He still didn't like suspecting their friend.

"What about Carl the Critter Curator?" he asked. "Why don't we question him next?"

"Because I'm still not sure about Carl," Frank admitted. "Even if he did know where we lived, how would he know you put Izumi outside?"

Joe gazed upward and said, "Because he was here?"

"What do you mean?" asked Frank.

Joe pointed up to a branch that had something purple dangling from it. Frank stepped up to it for a closer look.

"Hey," Frank said, freeing the object from the branch. "This looks like one of those buggy antennas Carl wore to the Earth Day Festival yesterday."

"It also means Carl was here," Joe said. "And left something behind."

"You mean his antenna?" Frank asked.

"That," Joe stated, "and proof!"

Chapter 6

UNDERCOVER DETECTIVES

"If it is Carl's antenna," Frank said, "how did it get up stuck in our tree?"

"Maybe Carl was walking under the tree and didn't feel the branch tear it off," Joe figured.

"I guess that makes sense," Frank agreed.

Excited, Joe smiled and said, "That means Carl was here. We ought to question him next instead of Phil!"

The brothers worked fast, pulling as many

weeds as they could find. When their chore was done, they hurried to the computer to search for Carl the Critter Curator's Insectarium. The new bug museum had been built behind the bigger Bayport Museum of Natural History.

"There's an 'opening gala' for the insectarium this afternoon at two," Frank said pointing to the screen.

"Carl would have to be at that!" Joe said.

Frank and Joe leaned forward as they read about the gala. There would be party snacks from a place called the Bug Appétit Café. There would also be an unveiling of the insectarium's most unique specimen—a giant beetle!

"Frank, Carl's got a beetle!" Joe said. "You know what that means?"

"Yeah," Frank said. "Next stop: the insectarium!"

It was a warm spring afternoon, so Frank and Joe rode their bikes to Carl the Critter Curator's Insectarium after getting permission from their mom. They would attend the opening gala and see the beetle with their own eyes.

But after they parked their bikes and approached the entrance . . .

"Sorry, boys," a woman told them. "This party is for adults only."

"You mean kids can't go?" Frank asked.

"Your flyer says to bring the kids," Joe said, "And as you can see, we're kids!"

Pinned on the woman's black-and-yellow bee-striped dress was a name tag reading LINDSAY.

"Kids can come any other day," Lindsay said with a smile. "Just not today."

Joe frowned until he remembered something in his pocket. He smiled at Lindsay and said, "Oh, actually, we're not here for the gala. We're here to give Carl the Critter Curator this!"

He pulled out the purple buggy antenna and held it up. When Lindsay saw it, she said, "Carl must have lost that. If you give it to me, I'll make sure he gets it."

"We'd like to give it to Carl, please," Frank blurted.

"So we can see his happy face when he gets it

back," added Joe. "It'll make our trip here worth-while!"

Confused, Lindsay just nodded. "Fine," she said. "Give Carl the antenna but leave right after, deal?"

"Deal!" Frank and Joe said in unison.

Lindsay stepped aside as the brothers entered the insectarium. A short hallway led to a main room, where fancily dressed guests chatted among glass tanks filled with live bugs.

"This place is so cool!" Joe said. "But I don't see Carl!"

"Forget about finding Carl," said Frank. "Let's look for that beetle."

"Frank, wait!" Joe said. He pointed to a flowing chocolate fountain in the middle of the room. "How can they have something yummy like that and not invite kids?"

Before Frank could stop him, Joe hurried over to the fountain. Liquid chocolate flowed from the top to the bottom, but something was missing.

"I don't see any pretzels or marshmallows to dip in the chocolate," Joe said. "Not even fruit!"

"We're not here to eat, Joe," Frank whispered. "We're here to look for—"

"Grasshoppers? Crickets?" a voice said.

The brothers turned to see a man dressed in a white jacket and holding a silver tray. Spread on the tray were dried insects—much like the crispy crunchy kind Leif had to feed his plants!

"Bugs?" Frank gulped.

"You want us to eat them?" asked Joe.

"You can use a toothpick to dip them in the chocolate," the server explained. "Insects are a great source of protein and quite tasty."

"No, thank you," Frank said. "But if you know where we can find a giant beetle—"

"No beetles are being served today," the server cut in. "Instead, may I suggest the mealworm meatballs or buggy burritos? Phyllis should be out with them in a minute."

"I'll pass, thanks," Joe said. "I think I'm coming down with a . . . bug."

As the brothers walked away from the fountain, Frank asked, "Do you really feel sick, Joe?"

"Only from imagining chocolate-covered bugs," Joe admitted. "I'll feel a lot better when we find Izumi."

The adult guests were too busy chatting and

snacking to notice there were two kids in the room. While Frank and Joe looked for Izumi, they found bugs behind glass in their natural environments and interactive insect games.

"Check it out, Joe," Frank called, stopping at the entrance to a darkened room. "Here's something called the Butterfly Cave, but I don't think Izumi would be there."

"He may not be there," Joe's voice called. "But I think I found him here."

"Where?" asked Frank.

He looked around until he saw something tall, completely covered with a white cloth. Underneath the cloth were two feet wearing Joe's sneakers!

Frank shot over to them and slipped underneath the cloth. He found Joe standing close up against a tall white pedestal. "What are you doing under here?" he whispered.

"Don't say a word," Joe replied. "Just look!"

He pointed his chin toward the top of the pedestal. On it was a clear plastic dome. Underneath the dome was a huge multi-legged beetle!

"How do we know that's Izumi?" Frank whispered. "I don't see his samurai helmet."

"That's because his head is under that little plant inside," Joe pointed out. "If I could just turn him around so we can see . . ."

Still under the cloth, Joe lifted the dome with one hand and picked up the beetle with his other. After turning the bug around, he said, "No helmet on this big guy. He may be a beetle, but he's not Izumi."

"He's not even the same color as Izumi," said Frank. "Put him back and let's get out of here before—"

"Friends of insects and honored guests," a voice boomed through the room. "Welcome to the gala opening of Carl the Critter Curator's Insectarium. In case you haven't guessed already . . . I am Carl!"

Frank and Joe stood motionless underneath their tented hideaway.

"I think we found Carl," Frank whispered.

"Yeah," Joe whispered back. "And if he pulls this cloth off—he's going to find us!"

Chapter 7

INSTANT MESSAGE

Joe held the beetle in one hand, the dome in the other. He and Frank tried not to move underneath the cloth while Carl continued to speak.

"Now I'd like to introduce the insectarium's pride and joy," Carl's voice said. "Please give a swarm welcome to—"

With a dramatic swoop, Carl yanked the cloth off the pedestal. Guests gasped when they saw Joe holding the beetle with Frank at his side.

"Hi," said Frank, forcing a smile.

"We were just leaving," Joe blurted. He was about to put the beetle back on the pedestal when—

SQUIIIIIIRT!

"Gross!" Joe yelled. He quickly put the beetle back on the pedestal and replaced the cover. Then he squeezed his nose. "What's that smell?"

"It's coming from the bug!" Frank said, clapping his hand over his own nose. "Bleeech!"

The stink cloud made its way from the beetle to the guests. Gagging and holding their noses, they headed for the exit.

"Wait, everyone, please!" Carl called out. "What do you expect from a beetle in the genus *Eleodes*?"

"Genus . . . what?" asked Joe.

Carl turned to the boys. "Better known as a stink beetle," he explained. "Quigley doesn't bite, but he sprays when provoked."

Joe let go of his nose. "I guess I provoked Quigley," he sighed. "Sorry."

"What were you boys doing under there anyway?" Carl asked.

"We were looking to see if Quigley was Izumi," Frank explained. "We heard you say you wanted a beetle for the insectarium."

"Izumi?" Carl asked. "You mean the Belly Bump boy's bug?"

Joe nodded and said, "After Aki's beetle disappeared from our doorstep, we found this."

Joe pulled out the purple antenna. Carl smiled.

"So that's what happened to the missing one," he said. "I wore my bug antennas to my book club meeting last night."

"Book club meeting?" Frank asked.

"Trudy Hardy's book club meeting," Carl confirmed. "The other members thought my bug antennas on Earth Day were a hoot."

"Wait," Joe said. "Did you say Trudy Hardy?"

Carl nodded, then left to coax guests back into the room. Frank and Joe immediately discussed what they'd heard.

"Aunt Trudy did have a book club meeting last night," Frank said. "Carl could have come to our house for that."

"Unless he just told us he went to the meeting," Joe said, "but came to our house to get Izumi instead."

Frank had an idea how to know for sure. After getting Carl's attention, he asked, "Could you tell us what book you talked about at the meeting, and what snacks you ate?"

"We're reading *The Great Gnatsby*," Carl replied. "And we ate the most delicious cookies shaped like flowers and bugs."

He cracked a smile and said, "If anyone knows how to celebrate Earth Day, it's Trudy!"

The brothers were satisfied with Carl's answer. The book and the cookies checked out. But Joe had one more question. . . .

"If you wanted a beetle like Izumi, Carl," Joe asked, "why did you settle for Mr. Stink over there?"

"There wasn't enough time to order a stag beetle from the bug farm," Carl explained. "So when I found Quigley crawling under my sink, the rest was history. Or should I say . . . *hssss*-tory!"

Frank and Joe laughed.

"Why don't you boys stay for some crispy critters?" Carl asked, "The servers will be rolling out caramel cricket cheesecake any minute!"

"Caramel cricket cheesecake?" Joe gulped.

"Um . . . no thanks, Carl," Frank said. "We still have to look for Izumi."

The brothers dashed out of the insectarium. Time was running out! But Joe made sure to cross Carl the Critter Curator's name from their suspect list before climbing onto his bike.

"Now Phil is our only suspect," Joe said with a frown.

"Hopefully Phil didn't take Izumi," Frank said. "All we have to do is rule him out."

"Then we'll have no more suspects," Joe said as he pocketed their clue book. "Zero. Zip. Zilch."

The brothers rode their bikes home. After parking them in the garage, they entered the house through the kitchen door. Their mother was by the fridge, unpacking bags of groceries. Joe noticed a red light flashing on the phone.

"Mom, someone's got a message," he pointed out.

"Thanks, Joe, I hadn't noticed," Mrs. Hardy said. "Who called?"

Joe leaned over the counter to check out the ID.

"There's a number but no name," he said. "Whoever it was called at seven thirty this morning."

"Your dad likes to turn down the ringer on weekends so the phone doesn't wake us up," Mrs. Hardy explained. "Go ahead and play the message."

"Okay, Mom," Frank said, teasing Joe by pressing the play button first. Joe was about to complain when Phil's voice said, "Hi, guys. I'm on my way to the inventors contest. And I even found a new good luck charm. Woo-hoo!"

The message ended. Frank and Joe stared at the phone, then at each other. Had Phil said "good luck charm"?

"I know we don't like to suspect friends," Frank said. "But I am so suspecting Phil right now!"

MATINEE DISMAY

"We've got to go to Phil's house, Frank," Joe said. "Right now."

"Not so fast, guys," Mrs. Hardy said. "We have tickets to see *Space Dudes* later. After the movie we're going out to dinner, remember?"

The brothers stared at their mother. How could they have forgotten? They had wanted to see *Space Dudes* for weeks!

"Aki isn't coming until tomorrow afternoon,"

Frank told Joe. "We can get Izumi back from Phil in the morning."

At four o'clock that afternoon, the Hardys piled into the family car. Once they were at the Bayport Cineplex, Frank and Joe stood in line for popcorn while their parents waited for them at their seats.

"Does Dad like caramel or cheese?" asked Joe. "Or the spicy kind?"

"None of those," Frank said as the line moved slowly toward the counter. "He likes buttered—"

"Hi, guys!" a voice said.

Frank and Joe froze. They'd know that voice anywhere. It was—

"A-Aki?" Joe stammered as he and Frank turned.

Aki stood on the side of the line, a big smile on his face. "Are you going to see *Ninja Rabbit*?" he asked.

"*Space Dudes*," both brothers chorused flatly.

Please don't ask about Izumi, Joe thought.

Please don't ask about Izumi, Frank thought.

"I'm glad I ran into you!" Aki said. "I miss Izumi too much. I want to come to your house after the movie and pick him up."

"No!" Joe cried a bit too loudly. "I mean—after the movie we're going for burgers."

"We're going to dinner too," said Aki. "I'll ask my dad to drive me to your house after we eat—"

"No!" Frank cut in. "I mean, after dinner we're going for dessert!"

"It's a place where you bake your own pies!" Joe added. "We'll be home crazy-late!"

Aki raised an eyebrow. "If Izumi is home alone all that time," he said, "then I really want him back tonight."

Frank and Joe traded desperate looks. Their excuses weren't working. They would have to go with the direct approach. . . .

"Aki, can we please keep Izumi until tomorrow afternoon?" Frank asked.

"You kind of promised," said Joe.

The brothers held their breath while Aki thought for a moment. He then nodded and said, "Promises are important. I'll be at your house tomorrow at three thirty sharp. Izumi should be in his tank and ready to go."

"You got it!" Joe blurted.

The brothers heaved sighs of relief as Aki walked across the lobby to join his family.

"A place where you bake your own pies?" Frank asked Joe. "Seriously?"

"I had to come up with something," Joe said as they finally reached the counter. "Now what kind of popcorn does Dad like?"

Space Dudes was awesome. So was dinner at the new veggie burger place that Joe had won a gift card to. He even admitted that kale burgers were pretty good!

But the next morning all Frank and Joe wanted to do was head straight to Phil's house. Was Izumi the lucky charm he'd brought to the Junior Inventors Challenge? They had to find out!

"I know I said I hope Phil doesn't have Izumi," Joe said as they headed over to Phil's house. "But after seeing Aki yesterday, I sure hope he does."

As they turned the corner onto Phil's block, Joe said, "There's one thing I don't get. How would Phil know that I put Izumi outside on our doorstep?"

"He wouldn't have to know," Frank said. "He could have come over Saturday morning to say hi and seen Izumi."

"Before seven thirty in the morning?" asked Joe. "That was the time of his message."

"The early bird catches the worm," Frank said with a shrug. "Or in this case, the stag beetle."

The brothers reached Phil's house and saw Mr. Cohen working on his car. "Phil isn't home now, guys," he said. "His mom enrolled him in Pretzel Kids on Sundays. Some yoga class."

"Oh," Frank said, disappointed.

"We can come back a little later," said Joe.

"Or wait in Phil's inventor's workshop," Mr. Cohen suggested. "If you do, you'll meet his unusual new pet!"

Unusual new pet?

Could Phil's unusual new pet be a lucky stag beetle? There was only one way to find out. . . .

"Thanks, Mr. Cohen," Frank said. "We would like to wait for Phil in his workshop!"

Chapter 9

SPEW CLUE

Phil's workshop was set up inside a toolshed in the Cohens' backyard. A homemade sign on the door read GENIUS AT WORK!

The door was half-open, so the brothers slipped inside. The workshop was filled with all kinds of gadgets and gizmos that he'd invented and built himself.

"Where are we going to find Izumi's tank in all this stuff?" Joe asked.

"I found something already," said Frank. "Look."

Joe saw Frank holding a badge from the Junior Inventors Challenge. Phil's name was on the badge as well as the location and time.

"The contest was held yesterday in Cedarville," Frank pointed out. "At nine o'clock in the morning."

"Cedarville is a long way from here," Joe said. "Phil would have had to have left super early to get there on time."

"Phil called us super early yesterday," Frank said, still studying the badge. "At seven thirty, remember?"

Joe didn't answer. Frank looked up from the badge to see his brother standing next to a familiar robot.

"Frank, it's Munchy!" said Joe. "I wonder how Phil got him to eat my pizza the other day."

"Don't press any buttons, Joe," Frank warned. But it was already too late. Joe had pressed what he thought was the start button and—

PHOO—PHOO—SPLAT!

The brothers yelped as green and brown mush spewed from Munchy's mouth!

"Joe, turn it off!" Frank shouted.

"I would if I knew how!" Joe shouted back.

The projectile mush hit the walls and landed in glops on the floor. Frank and Joe frantically searched for the off button until they heard a high squealing noise. It came from a small pink pig scurrying into the shed!

Munchy still spewed mush-rockets. But all the brothers could do was gawk at the pig as it feasted on a gloppy puddle.

"I think we found Phil's unusual new pet," Frank said.

"Yeah," said Joe. "And it's not a stag beetle."

Phil raced in next, shouting, "Hey! What's happening? What are you doing?"

"Trying to stop your robot," Frank said. "Can you give us a hand?"

Phil groaned, dropping his rolled-up yoga mat. He raced over to Munchy and snapped open a compartment to reveal three more buttons. He pressed one and Munchy's mouth clamped shut.

"So . . . what did I do wrong?" asked Joe.

"You pressed the eject button, that's what," Phil said. "It made Munchy spit out the compost."

"Sorry, Phil," said Joe.

"We were looking for Aki's beetle, Izumi," Frank

said. "We had him for the weekend until he disappeared."

"You mean the lucky bug?" Phil asked. "Why
would he be in here?"

"You wanted good luck for the contest," Frank
explained. "You also left a message saying you had a
lucky charm."

Phil nodded and said, "I called you from my
dad's phone on the way to the contest. But my lucky
charm wasn't the beetle."

Joe pointed to the pig and said, "You mean it was
the oinkster?"

"You bet!" said Phil with a grin. "Meet Pinky, a miniature potbellied pig."

"Since when are pigs good luck?" Joe asked.

"To some they are," Phil explained. "I borrowed Pinky from my cousin's farm. He said I could keep him as long as I wanted."

Phil looked down at Pinky and sighed. "I think I'll return him, though."

"Because he wasn't good luck?" asked Frank.

"No," Phil replied, "Because he's a total mess!"

Joe wrinkled his nose as Pinky smeared compost across the floor with his snout. "How did you take him all the way to Cedarville?" he asked.

"My parents wouldn't let me take Pinky to the contest," Phil replied, "but I won third prize anyway!"

"Awesome, Phil!" Frank exclaimed.

"What did you win?" asked Joe.

"Two weeks at Camp Galileo," Phil said. "It's not the whole summer, but I'll take it."

With a loud snort, Pinky scampered out of the workshop. Frank and Joe helped wipe up the mess with wads of paper towels. When they got most of it off the walls and floor, the brothers said goodbye to Phil.

"I'm glad Phil didn't take Izumi," Frank said as they walked away from the Cohen house.

"I'm glad he's not our *who* too," Joe said, before taking out their clue book. "But now we have no more suspects. And Aki will be by in a few hours!"

"I know, I know," Frank groaned. "What are we going to tell him?"

Glumly the brothers walked home. Halfway there, Joe stopped to point at a truck parked on the street. "Frank," he said. "Check it out."

Frank stopped to see where Joe was pointing. The truck belonged to Stan's Pest Control. On the side of the truck was a picture of a floppy-eared beagle. Under the dog were the words LET MR. SNIFF SNIFF OUT YOUR BEDBUGS!

"What do you think, Frank?" Joe asked. "Don't we know that dog?"

THE HARDY BOYS—and
YOU!

CAN YOU SOLVE THE MYSTERY OF THE MISSING STAG BEETLE?

Grab a piece of paper and write down your answers.
Or just turn the page to find out!

1. Frank and Joe ruled out Leif Bloomquist, Carl the Critter Curator, and their friend Phil Cohen. Can you think of anyone else who might have taken Izumi?

2. When Izumi is missing, the brothers suspect he was bug-napped. Why couldn't Izumi have crawled away from the Hardys' doorstep?

3. Joe spots Mr. Sniff's picture on the side of a truck. If Mr. Sniff is a bedbug sniffer, why would he be a clue to the missing beetle?

Chapter

10

BUG HUG

"Mr. Sniff is Lester's dog," Frank said. "But what's his picture doing on that truck?"

"And how can Mr. Sniff be Lester's dog," Joe wondered, "and Stan the exterminator's dog too?"

The boys found Stan at the back of the truck, busy removing equipment.

"Could you please tell us about Mr. Sniff?" asked Frank.

Stan smiled and said, "Mr. Sniff was the best. He

didn't just sniff bedbugs, but cockroaches, silverfish, beetles—"

"Beetles?" Frank and Joe chorused.

"Mr. Sniff could sniff a beetle five blocks away," Stan said proudly. "He's retired now, so we have a new bug sniffer."

Stan whistled, and a mixed-breed dog jumped out of the truck. "Meet Louise," he said. "She's new but learning fast!"

"If Mr. Sniff isn't working anymore, where did he go?" Joe asked.

"He's living with a nice family here in Bayport," Stan said. "They have a kid named Chester . . . Fester . . . Lester! Yeah, Lester, that's his name!"

Frank and Joe traded a satisfied look. The dog on the truck was Lester's!

Stan closed and locked the back of his truck. He said goodbye to Frank and Joe, picked up his equipment, then walked with Louise to a nearby house.

"Mr. Sniff was helping Lester with his Tadpole Scout scavenger hunt," Joe told Frank excitedly. "Maybe it was a bug scavenger hunt!"

"Mr. Sniff is a bug sniffer," Frank said. "Remember how he jumped up on Leif at the Earth Day Festival?"

"Yeah," said Joe. "We thought he sniffed out Leif's plant, but I'll bet he was sniffing the jar of bugs in his pocket!"

"Do you think Mr. Sniff had anything to do with Izumi's disappearance?" Frank asked.

"Lester lives next door," Joe said. "He could have walked by our house and Mr. Sniff sniffed Izumi on our doorstep!"

"Mr. Sniff could have led Lester straight to Izumi," Frank added. "And if Lester needed a beetle for his scavenger hunt—"

"He might have taken him!" Joe cut in. "Frank, our *who* could be Lester!"

Frank and Joe were about to hurry to Lester's house when two kids wearing Tadpole Scout uniforms walked by them.

"Hey, guys?" Joe called to them. "The Tadpole Scouts just had a scavenger hunt, right?"

"Yup," one scout said as they paused in front of Frank and Joe.

"What kind of scavenger hunt was it?" asked Joe.

The other scout pulled a paper out of his pocket. He held it up and said, "See for yourself."

The brothers stared wide-eyed at a list of six bugs.

It was a bug scavenger hunt, and the last one on the list was—

"A beetle!" Frank said.

"We're late," said the scout, folding his list. "Can we go to our meeting now?"

"As long as you take us with you!" said Frank with a smile.

He and Joe followed the scouts to Bay Street. The meeting was held in a big room above a shoe store. Once inside, the brothers checked out the kids. Most of them were at the snack table, drinking juice and eating chips. Only one scout sat in a chair, a big plastic bin on his lap. It was Lester!

"Hi, Lester," Frank said as he and Joe approached their neighbor.

"You're not Tadpole Scouts," Lester said. "What are you doing here?"

"We want to see what's in that container you're holding," said Joe. "Could it be bugs?"

Lester blinked rapidly, then murmured, "Maybe."

"Whatever's in there, Lester, can we just peek?" Frank asked.

"No," said Lester, hugging the bin close to him. "Step away from my bugs—I mean, stuff!"

"So you do have bugs in there!" Joe said as he grabbed the edge of the bin. "Is one of them the beetle from our doorstep?"

Lester stood up to get a stronger grip. "I don't know what you're talking about!" he insisted.

"Then let us look," Joe said, giving another tug.

"Joe, don't pull so hard at that," Frank warned him, "It might—"

PLUNK!! The bin dropped to the floor, and the lid popped off. Bugs of all kinds crawled out, scurrying everywhere!

"Bugs on the loose!" another Tadpole Scout shouted.

"Keep them away from the chips and dip!" someone else cried.

Lester glared at Joe. "See what you did?" he demanded. "It took Mr. Sniff and me days to catch those things!"

The Tadpole Scout leader hurried over to Lester. "Are those your bugs?" he asked.

"Yes," Lester admitted. "They're for the scavenger hunt."

"Lester, you didn't have to catch the bugs for the scavenger hunt," the scout leader explained. "All you had to do was take pictures of them!"

To prove it, the scouts held up pictures of bugs!

"Pictures?" Lester groaned. "Now you tell me!"

Frank turned to Joe and said, "We have to look for Izumi!"

The brothers ran around the room, looking for Izumi among the scattering bugs. They found a ladybug, grasshopper, even a spider, but no beetle. Until . . .

Hsss . . . hssss . . . hssss.

Joe froze in his tracks. That was the same noise that had kept him awake the other night!

Frank was searching through a closet for bugs while Joe followed the hissing noise. It brought him to the snack table, where he spotted a big beetle. It was slowly crawling onto the chip-and-dip set!

Joe stepped closer to the table. The beetle was black and shiny and looked like it was wearing a samurai helmet.

"Frank!" Joe exclaimed, picking up the bug. "I think I found him!"

Frank hurried over to Joe and the beetle.

"He looks like Izumi," said Frank. "But is he?"

"There's only one person here who can tell us," Joe said. He held the beetle gently as he and Frank walked back to Lester.

"Lester, did you take this beetle off our door step?" Frank asked him.

"We just want to know the truth," said Joe. "And aren't all Tadpole Scouts supposed to be honest?"

Lester gave his troop leader a sideways glance. "I guess," he sighed.

"So?" Frank asked. "Did you take Izumi or not?"

"I borrowed him!" Lester insisted. "Mr. Sniff found the beetle at your house Saturday morning. I was going to keep him until after I got my bug badge today."

The frazzled scout leader raced over to toss more bugs into Lester's bin. "Give the beetle back, Lester," he said. "You earned your bug badge for the scavenger hunt!"

"I did? Yes!" Lester cheered. He turned to the brothers and said, "Izumi's tank is in my room if you want to come get it."

"You bet we do!" Frank said, looking at the clock on the wall. "Aki will be at our house in half an hour!"

Lester left the scoutmaster and his troop trying to catch the rest of the bugs and followed the Hardys outside. They hurried back to the Lopez house, where Lester returned Izumi's tank.

"Home sweet home, Izumi!" Joe said after placing him into his tank and closing the lid. "Now let's get you back to Aki!"

Aki was already waiting on the Hardys' doorstep when Frank and Joe reached their house. "Hey, guys," he said as he waved them over. "Where's Izumi?"

Joe grinned and pulled the tank out from under his arm. He held it up and sang, "Ta-daaa!"

"Izumi!" Aki exclaimed. He took the tank from Joe and hugged it to his chest. He took off the lid and lifted his beetle from the tank. "He looks happy . . . but why does he smell like barbecue potato chips?"

"Sorry, Aki," Frank sighed. "I know we made a lot of excuses, but Izumi was kind of . . . lost."

"Lost—and found!" Joe declared.

Aki smiled, glad to have his pet back. "When Izumi wasn't lost," he asked, "did he bring you good luck?"

"Not sure about that," Joe told Aki. "But I think he brought us a new friend."

That night Joe was happy to write the last two *W*s in the clue book. *Who* was Lester—right next door. *Why* was to win the Tadpole Scouts scavenger hunt and his bug badge.

"Maybe we should have a bug as a pet, Frank," Joe said, looking up from the clue book.

"As long as it doesn't bite," said Frank.

"There's only one bug that can bite us," Joe said with a grin. "The detective bug!"

With that he wrote in big letters: *CASE CLOSED!*

THE FIVE W's

Who: Carl? Phil? Leif?

What: Izumi's gone!

Where: on the doorsteps

When: between 10:30pm & 8:00am

Why: to win the scout badge

LESTER!

CASE CLOSED!

HELP DECODE CLUES AND SOLVE MYSTERIES WITH THE THIRD-GRADE DETECTIVES!

The Clue of the
Left-Handed Envelope

The Puzzle of the
Pretty Pink Handkerchief

The Mystery of the
Hairy Tomatoes

The Cobweb Confession

The Riddle of the
Stolen Sand

The Secret of the
Green Skin

Case of the Dirty Clue

Secret of the
Wooden Witness

The Case of the
Bank-Robbing Bandit

The Mystery of the
Stolen Statue

FROM ALADDIN
KIDS.SIMONANDSCHUSTER.COM

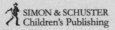